Praise for
Flim Flam & Other Such Gobbledygook

"Children love playing with words like *gobbledygook*, *flim flam*, and *fiddle-dee-dee*. With its gentle good humor, rhyme, and clever illustrations, this story of a barnyard party enthralls kids while teaching the importance of choosing inclusion over cliques. It invites children to leave their poppycock behind and join in the fun of respecting uniqueness—with a loud doodle-doo."

—Lehua Parker, author of the Niuhi Shark Saga trilogy

"In her delightful verse, Melica Hudgens treats her readers to a fanciful visit to the barnyard, with the rhythm of her rhyming words as well as the large, colorful pictures. We love meeting the characters who live there and seeing their feelings about other animals who could be invited to the big barnyard party. We are not only entertained but also gently instructed. This book promises to be a big favorite for children and the adults who read to them! Hooray for this latest book in Cedar Fort's excellent children's picture book collection!"

—Margaret D. Nadauld, author of *A Mother's Influence: Raising Children to Change the World* and *Write Back Soon: Letters of Love and Encouragement for Young Women*; grandmother of many; and retired English teacher

FLIM FLAM
& OTHER SUCH GOBBLEDYGOOK

By Melica Hudgens · ILLUSTRATED BY Jay Fontano

Sweetwater Books | An Imprint of Cedar Fort, Inc. | Springville Utah

ISBN 13: 978-1-4621-1684-3

Published by Sweetwater Books, an imprint of Cedar Fort, Inc.
2373 W. 700 S., Springville, UT, 84663
Distributed by Cedar Fort, Inc., www.cedarfort.com

LIBRARY OF CONGRESS CATALOGING-IN-PUBLICATION DATA

Hudgens, Melica, 1960- author.
Flim flam and other such gobbledygook / written by Melica Hudgens ; illustrated by Jay Fontano.
     pages cm
Summary: One morning after the animals finish cleaning up the barnyard, Edwin Rooster suggests getting everyone together for a party.
ISBN 978-1-4621-1684-3 (hard back : alk. paper)
[1. Stories in rhyme. 2. Domestic animals--Fiction. 3. Kindness--Fiction. 4. Parties--Fiction.] I. Title.
PZ8.3.H8559Fl 2015
[E]--dc23
                          2014045721

Cover and page design by Michelle May
Cover design © 2015 by Lyle Mortimer
Edited by Justin Greer

Printed and bound in China

10 9 8 7 6 5 4 3 2 1

Printed on acid-free paper

All the Barnyard was a-flutter;
they'd Done their Chores—
thrown out the Clutter.

Edwin Rooster and Clara Hen
saw that it was half past ten.

Edwin said, "The work is done—
let's plan a party and have some fun!

We'll meet out by the swimming hole
beside our favorite grassy knoll."

"But who will come?" poor Clara cried.
She shook her head, sat down, and sighed.

"Our neighbors here of fur and feather
don't much like to be together.
They think the others are faulty or flawed,
strange or imperfect, ugly or odd."

EDWIN SAID IN A HOPEFUL WAY,
"MAYBE THEY'LL CHANGE THEIR MINDS TODAY.

"We'll Plan the Party and have a Blast.
How long can their old grudges last?"

Then Clara said, "Come on, let's go.
If we don't ask, we'll never know."

They first ran into Purdy Pig
and told her all about the gig.

Purdy paused—and said, "It depends
precisely on who else attends.

"Some of our neighbors are stinky, you see,
and I don't want them close to me."

Clara cried, "Now listen to me;
our barnyard friends are as clean as can be."

Anna Cow heard their chat
as she munched on her hay.
She swallowed and said,
"I have something to say."

She rolled her eyes and said with a sneer,
"Too many puppies run wild around here.
Always barking—they're noisy and rude.
The hubbub they cause puts me in a bad mood."

Right then, Jonder Dog, with his young 'uns, walked by
and said with his nose pointed up to the sky,
"You see, only three of the puppies are mine.
Tombo's the guilty one; he has nine!"

Delia Duck said, "Don't invite Maynard Horse. His knees are too bumpy. His mane is too coarse." "Delia," said Edwin, "now that's silly chatter! If Maynard has bumpy knees, it doesn't matter.

"Stop all this twaddle! Let's get down to earth. Don't you know how much a friendship is worth?" Delia just looked at him straight in the eye— and said, "Give up, Edwin. It's foolish to try."

Then Edwin gave a loud DOODLE-DOO
to gather their big and their little friends too.

Edwin and Clara
stood on the fence.
Edwin said, "Welcome,
ladies and gents.

"We asked you to come to a party today,
but your uppity attitudes got in the way.
Friends and neighbors, let's take a look—
all this is nonsense and gobbledygook!

"Don't squawk if someone is different, unique—
with a patch of green hair, or a lump on his beak.

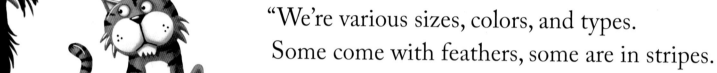

"We're various sizes, colors, and types.
Some come with feathers, some are in stripes.

"So, whether you're tall with a twitch or a scar,
if you walk with a limp, or your hair is bizarre,

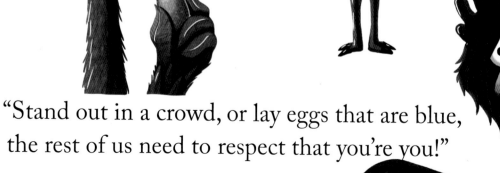

"Stand out in a crowd, or lay eggs that are blue,
the rest of us need to respect that you're you!"

The barnyard animals thought for a while— "Edwin is right!" they said with a smile.

Then, at the party,
they ate and they played.

They laughed together
and sat in the shade.

So if you hear flim flam or gobbledygook,
get rid of it quickly by hook or by crook!
Don't let it botch friendships or ruin your day.
Shoo it out! Hurry! It must go away.

And if you see someone who acts like a mule,
remember the animals and their new rule:

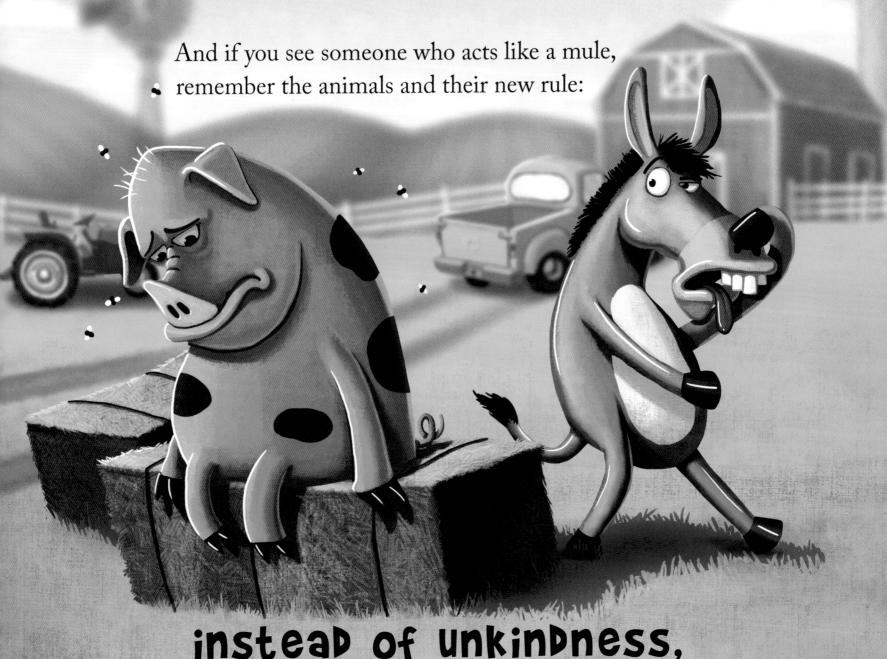

instead of unkindness,
choose niceness and see

exactly how joyful
the Barnyard Can Be!

glossary

a-flutter: in a state of excitement; flapping of wings

bizzare: strange or unusual in style or appearance

botch: bungle, spoil, or mess up

fiddle-de-dee: nonsense

flimflam: idle talk or nonsense, humbug

gig: a performance or get-together

gobbledygook: unintelligible jargon, gibberish, or mumbo jumbo

grudge: bad feelings for someone that you are not willing to let go of

hubbub: lots of noise, confusion, or disturbance

knoll: small hill or mound

nonsense: absurd or meaningless words or ideas; foolish conduct

poppycock: nonsense

silly chatter: senseless, ridiculous, or trivial talk

twaddle: useless or senseless writing or talk

uppity: arrogant, snobbish

ABout the Author

If she's not sitting at the computer writing, **Melica Hudgens** can usually be found out in the garden, pulling weeds or finding a place to plant something new.

After attending a dozen different schools and living in twice as many places, Hudgens says, "I've grown accustomed to meeting new people and making friends. My favorite pastime is visiting with people."

Melica also enjoys riding bicycles with her husband, taking walks, and enjoying the gifts of nature with her grandchildren.

ABout the Illustrator

As a young boy, **Jay Fontano** loved to watch cartoons and read comic strips in the newspaper. Now he works as an illustrator drawing funny pictures for T-shirts and illustrating books.

Jay and his wife have 6 children and enjoy spending time together camping, swimming, exploring, and having fun. They live near a creek close to the mountains with their dog Nacho and a small flock of chickens.

He still watches cartoons and reads comic strips.

For Lynn, with love and appreciation for your constant support and encouragement.
—M.H.

For Sassy: Thanks for keeping our Barnyard a joyful place.
—JF